Disney's KiM POSSIBLE

THE NEW RON

Adapted by Kiki Thorpe

Based on the series created by

Mark McCorkle & Bob Schooley

Watch it on
DISNEY CHANNEL
abc Kids

DISNEY PRESS

VOLO

New York

Printed in the United States of America

First Edition
1 3 5 7 9 10 8 6 4 2

Library of Congress Catalog Card Number: 2002095478

ISBN 0-7868-4488-4
For more Disney Press fun, visit www.disneybooks.com
Visit DisneyChannel.com

CHAPTER 1

Ron's New 'Do

This was it. The moment she had been waiting for. Kim Possible, world-class superspy and cheerleader extraordinaire, leaned forward in her chair. Her eyes shone with excitement.

Rufus, the naked mole rat, stood on the table. His whiskers twitched nervously as he watched and waited.

In the middle of Kim's kitchen, François, the famous French hairdresser, stood face-to-face with the greatest challenge of his lifetime. François had cut the curls of kings and queens. He'd trimmed the tresses of tyrants. He'd pouffed the hairdos of superstars. But never in all his years of snipping had he faced a feat as fearsome as this one. François trembled in his Italian leather boots. He placed his hand on his chin, trying to decide what to do.

"No!" he cried in a heavy French accent. "Even for me, it is too much."

"You can do it, François!" Kim cried. She smiled her best cheerleader smile.

A look of determination came into François's eyes. "You are right, Kim Possible," he said. "I must try."

François grabbed a comb and a pair of scissors off the table. Taking a deep breath, he raised his hands. And then . . .

Snip, snip, snip.

François began to cut Ron Stoppable's hair.

Kim's best friend, Ron, sat in a chair at her kitchen table. He had a plastic sheet tied around his neck like a giant bib. As pieces of blond hair flew from François's scissors, Ron looked nervously at Kim.

"K.P.? Are you sure about this?" he asked.

"Ron, François is an artist," Kim said. "Getting him to make a house call is, like, *epic.*"

"I could not visit the States and not help Kim Possible," François said, looking at Kim sincerely. "Not after what you did for my poodle."

Kim shrugged and laughed. "Those dog-nappers had it coming," she said.

Kim never liked to take credit for her good deeds, no matter how death-defying and majorly heroic they were.

Just then, Kim's mom, Dr. Possible, walked into the room. She was on her way to the Middleton hospital, where she worked as a brain surgeon. But she stopped when she saw the operation that was taking place right in her kitchen.

"Kimmie, why is Ron getting a haircut in our kitchen?" she asked.

"Because he ferociously needs one," Kim said.

"Oh, I don't know . . ." Kim's mom said.

"I do," said Kim. "I know what's best for Ron, even if he doesn't."

Studying Ron's hair closely, François asked, "So, Ronald, your old barber— he was some- what . . . vision- impaired?"

"No, he could see shapes," Ron said. "Kind of."

François began to snip faster. Big chunks of hair fell to the floor.

Kim's mom gasped. "He's really taking a lot off."

A look of panic crossed Ron's face. Rufus held his paws over his eyes.

"He'll thank me, Mom," Kim said. "It's no big."

Suddenly, François stopped snipping. He dipped his finger into a jar of gooey hair gel.

"The finale," François announced dramatically. "A pea-size dollop of Le Goop. As they say, the secret is in the sea urchin."

He rubbed the gel into Ron's hair. Then, with a final flick of the comb, François stepped back. Beaming with pride, he held a mirror up for Ron to see.

Ron looked at his reflection. His eyes opened wide.

"Aaaaaaaaaaaaaaaaaaaaaah!" he screamed.

CHAPTER 2

New 'Do Blues

"I'm telling you, it was a change for the better, Ron," Kim said later that morning at school. "Trust me."

"Don't play with me, Kim," Ron said. His voice was muffled because he was standing inside the janitor's closet. He'd been hiding there all morning.

"Just come out," Kim said impatiently.

Ron stepped out of the closet with a bucket over his head.

"Oh, that's *much* less embarrassing," Kim said.

Ron took the bucket off. He had a wool hat pulled tightly down over his hair.

"By making me get the foofy haircut, you've disrupted my core," Ron explained. "My identity. My essential Ron-ness."

"Ron-ness?" Kim asked.

"Yeah," Ron said. "That easygoing, devil-may-care attitude that makes me . . . uh . . . an easygoing, devil-may-care guy." He looked down at Rufus, who was hiding in his pants pocket. "Right, Rufus?" he said.

Rufus squealed in agreement.

"I had no idea there was so much to you, Ron," Kim said. "I'm sorry. I guess there's only one thing I can do."

Reaching over, Kim yanked the wool hat off Ron's head.

"New haircut!" she yelled. "Ron Stoppable got a new haircut!"

She dashed down the hallway, waving Ron's hat in the air. Ron yelped and covered his head with his hands.

"Give it, Kim!" he cried, chasing after his hat.

But as Ron rounded the corner, he skidded to a stop. Three pretty girls were standing in the middle of the hallway. And they were staring right at him.

But they weren't just *any* girls.

"Seniors!" Ron gasped. The seniors were the royalty of Middleton High. They practically ruled the school. Ron's face turned bright red. He took a step backward.

Suddenly, Amelia, the prettiest girl, stepped forward. If the seniors were royalty,

 Amelia was definitely queen.

"Do I know you?" she asked Ron.

"I'm, er, Stop Ronnable—er, Ron Stoppable," Ron stuttered.

"That's a very, very cool haircut, Ron Stoppable," Amelia said.

Ron was stunned. "Thanks," he squeaked.

"Maybe I'll see you later," Amelia said.

"Maybe. I mean, sure. Yeah. Later," Ron said. He watched as Amelia and her friends

walked away. "This haircut
rocks! Stadium rocks!" he
cried when they were gone.

But suddenly . . . *sproing!* Ron
felt something move on the back of his head.

He froze and slowly raised his eyes.

"Oh, no!" he moaned.

It was a cowlick.

Later that day, as Kim was leaving school,
she heard Ron's voice.

"Kim!" he whispered urgently. He peeked
out from behind a tree.

"Ron?" Kim said in surprise. She hadn't
seen him since she had taken his hat that
morning. "Where have you been all day?"
she asked.

Ron ignored her question. He didn't have
time for small talk. "Please tell me this haircut comes with a warranty," he begged.

Kim looked at Ron's face. It had *major*

disaster written all over it. "What happened?" she asked.

Ron looked both ways to make sure no one was coming. When the coast was clear, he stepped out from behind the tree. He pointed at the hair sticking up on the back of his head.

"Cowlick," he explained,

Ron smoothed down the hair. An instant later, it sprang up again.

Rufus scrambled onto Ron's head and bravely threw himself onto the cowlick, smashing it down.

"Way to go, Rufus!" Ron cheered.

Sproing! The cowlick popped back up, tossing Rufus into the air. Ron caught him and looked at Kim for help.

But Kim just shrugged. "It'll probably flatten out when your hair gets a little longer," she said.

"That's one scenario," Ron said, frowning. "Here's another one. We go to France. Find François. Get more Le Goop."

Kim stared at him. "Ron, are you suggesting that I call in a favor so you can go to France for *hair gel*?" she asked.

"Uh, *oui*," he said.

CHAPTER 3

Trouble in Paris

It was dark outside by the time Kim and Ron left François's shop in Paris. Kim waited at the door, tapping her foot impatiently. Ron was taking forever!

"So, you're saying I need a new wardrobe to take the hair to the next level?" Ron asked François. Ron's hair was freshly Le Gooped. The cowlick was nowhere in sight.

"Without question, Ronald," François replied. He eyed Ron's baggy cargo pants and made a *tsk-tsk* sound. "The hair. The clothes. They must harmonize."

"Done and done, François," Ron said.

Kim rolled her eyes. One thing was for sure. Ron's new haircut had certainly given him an attitude.

"*Merci!*" Ron said. François waved goodbye and closed the door of his shop.

As they turned to leave, a beautiful French woman walked past. Ron stared at her.

"*Bonjour!*" he called.

The woman turned her head and smiled at him. She blew a kiss over her shoulder.

Unfortunately, she didn't notice that she was walking right toward an underground metro station.

"Aieeeeeee!" the woman shrieked as she tumbled down the stairs.

Kim shook her head in amazement. "Have these people never seen hair before?" she asked.

Ron smiled knowingly. Kim couldn't stand it that he was getting all the attention for once. "Somebody's tweaked," he said.

"I'm not tweaked," Kim snapped.

"You *reek* tweak," said Ron.

Kim glared at him and raised her voice. "I find it very *annoying* that hair-care products have become the center of the universe," she said.

"Hair-care products have always been the center of the universe," Ron replied. "I just found out about it recently."

Ugh. Kim scowled at him in disgust. Let him find his own ride back to Middleton, she thought. Better yet, let him float home on his inflated ego. She turned to leave.

Suddenly, the lights in François's store went dark. A second later—*zzzt, zzzt, zzzt*—

19

one by one, the streetlights overhead also blinked out.

"Hmm?" Kim said.

She looked around. The brightly lit windows of the nearby apartment buildings suddenly darkened. Then the lights in an entire skyscraper shut down all at once.

Kim and Ron glanced at each other. Something wasn't right.

Together they turned and looked at the Eiffel Tower, France's most famous monument. Rows of lights ran up its sides. It shone like a giant Christmas tree.

But as they watched, the brilliant bulbs on the tower flickered once and then went out. The entire city of Paris was dark.

CHAPTER 4

A Draining Experience

"That's weird," said Ron.

"Yeah, it is," Kim agreed. "I'm calling Wade."

She pulled her Kimmunicator from her belt and dialed Wade. A second later, his chubby face appeared on the screen. Wade was the ten-year-old supergenius who ran Kim's Website. He could get info from anywhere in the world with a few taps on his computer keys.

"Paris is blacked out, Wade," Kim said. "What's the sitch?"

"Let me scan the news sites," Wade said. He hit a few keys on his computer. "Wow!" he exclaimed. "It's not just France. There are rolling blackouts all over Europe!"

"Maybe we can trace the drain," Kim said. "Can you patch the Kimmunicator into the European grid?"

Wade typed into his computer. In seconds, Kim's Kimmunicator was connected to the entire European energy system.

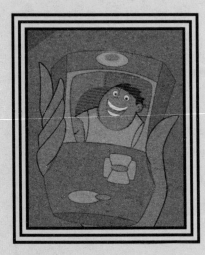

"Done," Wade told her.

"Great!" Kim said. "And we'll need transportation. . . ."

"No problem," Wade said. "I've done some consulting work for a French aeronautics firm. They'll help out."

Moments later, Kim and Ron were soaring over Europe in a pilotless helicopter. Wade was flying it by remote control from his bedroom.

Kim checked their coordinates on the Kimmunicator. They had just reached the Bay of Biscay, on the coast of Spain.

"I've traced the drain to eight degrees one minute west, forty-six degrees north," she told Wade. "But my map shows nothing out there."

Ron looked out the window.

"'Nothing' left its lights on," he said.

Kim looked where he was pointing. A brilliant light shone up from the dark water below.

"It's an island," Kim said. "Wade, take us down."

23

"Gently!" Ron yelped as the helicopter suddenly plunged.

The helicopter slowly descended and landed on the island's rocky shore. Kim and Ron climbed out and scrambled up a jagged cliff.

At the top, they stopped. "Whoa," said Ron.

The entire island was surrounded by a twenty-foot-high steel wall. Razor wire curled across the top, and lights blazed from the other side. Someone had gone to a lot of trouble to keep intruders off the island. But who? And why?

CHAPTER 5

The Seniors

Kim scanned the wall, looking for an entrance. But there wasn't so much as a peephole anywhere in sight.

Opening her backpack, Kim pulled out a hair dryer.

Only it wasn't really a hair dryer. When Kim flipped the power switch to HIGH, a grappling hook shot out from the dryer's nozzle. The hook flew over the top of the wall, trailing a rope behind it. Kim and Ron climbed up the rope to the top of the wall.

Suddenly, they were blinded by a brilliant glare. Outside it was night, but on the other side of the wall it was bright as day! Kim squinted up at what appeared to be the sun. Only it wasn't the sun—it was a lamp the size of an Olympic swimming pool!

"That's a really big lightbulb," Kim said.

"No wonder there's no power in Europe," said Ron.

Kim shielded her eyes and looked around. Beneath the giant lamp sat an enormous

house made of glass and chrome. A young man wearing a teeny bathing suit was lying next to one of the many swimming pools, sunbathing.

Kim jumped to the ground, pulling Ron behind her.

"Uh, hello?" she called to the young man.

The young man lifted his sunglasses and peeked out at her. "Father," he said loudly. "I see people. They must be the new servants."

Whoosh! Suddenly, the chrome doors slid open, and a man in his fifties stepped out. He had silver hair and very tan skin. Strangely, he was wearing ski clothes.

"Very good, very good," he said to Kim and Ron. "You have brought more lightbulbs?"

"Did you bring lightbulbs?" Ron whispered to Kim.

Kim stepped forward and held out her hand. "I'm Kim Possible," she said. "And this is Ron Stoppable."

The man shook her hand and smiled. "Welcome. Welcome to my home," he said. "We have only just turned everything on. I am Señor Senior, Sr. And this is my son, Señor Senior, Jr."

The young man in the teeny bathing suit stood up and smiled at them. He had big muscles, a movie-star tan, and a haircut that looked an awful lot like Ron's.

"Your haircut," he said to Ron. "It is very nice."

Ron ran a hand through his glistening locks. "I use Le Goop," he said.

"As do I," the young man replied.

He eyed Ron's baggy cargo pants and wrinkled his nose. "But your clothes. They do not harmonize."

"I know, I know," Ron said quickly. "I'm all over it, dude."

"I was just going to take a quick ski down my indoor mountain," the older man told them. "Care to join me?"

Indoor ski mountain? Ron's face lit up. But before he could reply, Kim shook her head. "No thank you, Señor. . . ."

"Senior, Sr.," he said. "Some refreshment perhaps? I have some lovely juice. Quite amazing, really. It comes in a box."

"A juice box would be nice," said Kim.

"I want to ski," Ron whispered. Kim elbowed him.

"Yeah, okay. Juice is good," Ron said.

A short time later, Ron had slurped the last drop from his juice box and sighed. He was bored.

Señor Senior, Jr., sighed, too. He drummed his fingers on the table. He was even more bored than Ron.

Only Señor Senior, Sr., was still paying attention to Kim.

"So, I guess what I'm saying is that energy is a precious resource," Kim explained. She handed the Seniors some conservation pamphlets. "It's up to each and every one of us to do our part. So, a little eco-awareness might be in order here."

Señor Senior, Sr., was fascinated. He'd never heard of such a thing! "I am but a simple multibillionaire," he said mod-

estly. "I can't believe that what I do has any effect on anyone."

Kim looked around the house. The Seniors not only had a massive sunlamp and an indoor ski mountain—they had a fish tank the size of a football stadium!

"Your house sucks up so much energy, it's causing blackouts all over Europe," Kim told Señor Senior, Sr.

"And these people without power—they are inconvenienced?" he asked.

"Very," Kim replied.

"You see, Junior?" Señor Senior, Sr., said. "How awful it is for the poor. But what can I do?"

Slightly irritated, Kim said, "For starters, you could turn off that giant sunlamp."

Junior leaped up from the table and glared at Kim. "But if I am to be a teen pop star, I need a robust tan!" he cried.

"There's a ton of things you can do to make your house more efficient," Kim told the Seniors.

"'House'?" Ron said suddenly. "It's more like a lair."

"Lair?" Señor Senior, Sr., frowned and shook his head. "I do not like the sound of that. Too . . . sinister."

"This place *screams* sinister," Ron said.

"It's on a private island that isn't on any map."

"I value my privacy," Señor Senior, Sr., replied.

"C'mon," Ron said. "Look at all the chrome." He pointed at the shiny metal doors that interlocked like jigsaw-puzzle pieces. "You've got doors that go *whoosh*."

Junior nodded. "I always wondered about the *whoosh*."

"I like the *whoosh*," Señor Senior, Sr., replied. "It is the door saying, 'I'm closed.'"

Kim scowled at Ron. "It's fine, sir. Ignore him," she told Señor Senior, Sr.

Ron didn't notice. He was too busy imag-

ining the perfect villain's lair. "All I'm saying is that a guy could take over the world from a place like this," he told Señor Senior, Sr.

Kim glared at her friend. The last thing she needed was someone else trying to take over the world.

"Wouldn't take much," Ron continued happily. "Maybe a communications system. Some missiles. Probably throw in some traps. You know, self-activating lasers, an indoor lagoon full of piranhas . . ."

"Why ever would we want piranhas?" Señor Senior, Sr., asked.

"To eat the good guys," Ron said. *Duh*.

Kim leaped up from her chair and dragged Ron toward the door. If Ron didn't shut up soon, she was going to personally feed him to the piranhas! "Just put in some fluorescents,"

she told Señor Senior, Sr. "That should do the trick."

"I'd also think about a secret underground grotto with a speedboat for escape purposes," Ron added enthusiastically. "And . . . and gigantic Spinning Tops of Doom!" Ron's face lit up. He was practically squealing with excitement. "They would be huge! And they'd destroy anything in their path!"

"Come on, Mr. Spinning Tops of Doom," Kim snapped. "I have homework."

She dragged Ron through the doorway and down toward the helicopter.

"Good-bye. Thank you," Señor Senior, Sr.,

called after them. He watched as their helicopter rose into the air.

"I hope the one with the nice haircut finds better trousers," Señor Senior, Jr., said.

"Yes," Señor Senior, Sr., replied absently. He was still thinking about what Ron had said. "But his ideas . . . I have so much money and free time. I could use a hobby."

A sinister gleam came into Señor Senior, Sr.'s dark eyes. He was getting an idea of his own.

CHAPTER 6

Food for Thought

At dinner the next night, Kim told her family about Señor Senior, Sr., and his enormous, energy-sucking house.

"I left him some pamphlets," Kim said.

"Well, all of you kids could stand to turn off a few lights," Kim's dad said from the head of the table.

Kim sighed and took a sip of water. Her dad wasn't a very good listener. He was a rocket scientist, and his mind was always in outer space.

"Dinner!" Kim's mom called from the kitchen. She walked into the dining room and placed a steaming dish on the table. "Ta-da!" she cried, lifting the lid.

In the middle of the plate was a lump of grayish meat that appeared to be a roasted . . .

"Brain! Cool!" Kim's ten-year-old brother Jim shouted, leaping up from his chair.

"I want a lobe!" his twin, Tim, cried, jumping up, too.

"Boys, please," their father said sternly.

"Sorry," Jim said. "May I *please* have a slice of steaming human brain?"

"Pleeeeeease?" Tim added.

"First, Ron. Now, my family," she groaned. "Has everyone lost their—*ew*!" Kim shuddered as her mother sliced into the brain. She couldn't even look at her dinner. "That is so gross," she said.

"Kimmie, it's just meat loaf," Mrs. Possible said. "I'm making it for the Neurosurgeons' Potluck. Thought I'd try it on you guys first."

"Kudos on the realism. Uncanny," Mr. Possible said enthusiastically. "So what's up with Ronald?" he asked, turning to Kim. "Something you want to talk about?"

"Yeah," Kim said. "But I guess I should be talking to him." Kim watched as her mom slid a slice of brain loaf onto her dad's plate. "May I be excused?" she asked.

"I'll save you a plate, honey," her mom said, as Kim dashed from the room.

In her room, Kim picked up her phone and dialed Ron's number. After a couple of rings, his answering machine picked up.

"Hey!" Ron's message said. "You've reached the home of Ron Stoppable and his fierce new haircut. Leave a message."

"How can Ron not be home?" Kim said to herself. Ron was *always* home. That is, unless he was with Kim. "Okay, better page him," she decided. She dialed another number.

At that moment, Ron was in a dressing room at L'Homme Plastique, an ultratrendy clothing store in the Middleton Mall. He was looking for an outfit to match his cool new hair.

Kim's call came through on Ron's beeper, but Ron didn't hear it. His beeper was buried beneath a pile of clothes, on the dressing-room floor.

Suddenly, Rufus popped up from the pile. He'd been buried under the pile of clothes, too! Rufus held up the beeper and squealed, trying to get Ron's attention.

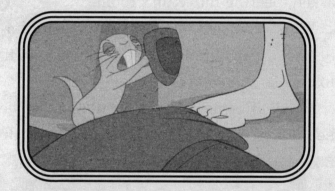

Ron was too busy trying on shirts to notice. He pulled off another shirt and tossed it to the floor. It landed on Rufus's head. Rufus sighed sadly.

On the other side of town, Kim sighed,

too, and hung up the phone. Maybe Ron had been right after all, she thought. Maybe the new haircut had been a really big mistake. Who could have known that a new 'do could turn her lovable Ron-ster into a raging ego monster?

Just then Kim's dad came up the stairs. "You and Ronald all squared away?" he asked, peering into Kim's room.

"No," Kim said. "I can't even reach him." She sat up on her bed. "Dad, did you ever try to change somebody?"

Her dad came and sat on the end of her bed. "Well, not a human," he replied. "But

back in grad school there was this lab rat. Pinky-Joe Curlytail I called him. Poor little guy was always running mazes for those psych majors." Dr. Possible clenched his fists. "How I hated them. . . ." he muttered.

"Dad," Kim interrupted. "What does this have to do with me?"

"Well, it seemed to me that Pinky-Joe Curlytail was just so helpless," Dr. Possible explained. "I constructed a tiny cybertronic battle suit."

Kim stared at him. "For the *rat*?" she asked. Even for her dad, this was way out.

"No more mazes for him," her dad said cheerfully. He patted Kim's head and stood up to leave. But at the door, he paused. "In retrospect, giving him a working plasma blaster probably went too far," he admitted. "Blew up half the science building. Rampaged across campus." Dr. Possible chuckled. "Oh, Pinky-Joe," he said fondly.

"So, this creating-a-monster thing runs in the family," Kim muttered. She should have known better than to ask her dad for advice. Defeated, Kim fell back onto her bed and closed her eyes.

CHAPTER 7

The New and Improved Ron

When Ron walked down the hallway the next day, everyone stared. Sophomore girls fluttered their eyelashes. Junior girls smiled and sighed. Even the senior girls watched the new Ron Stoppable strut down the hall in his cool new digs.

Kim didn't notice all the fuss. She had her head inside her locker, looking for her homework. Ron came up behind her.

"What's happenin', Mama?" he purred.

"Oh, hey," Kim said, turning around. "Where were you last night? I paged you and . . ."

Whoa! Ron's usual sneakers, fuzzy sweater, and baggy cargo pants were gone. In their place he was wearing a fancy blue mock turtleneck, shiny leather ankle boots, and . . . were those *pleather* pants?

"What happened to you?" Kim asked in amazement.

Ron smiled and cocked one of his eyebrows. "Ron Stoppable has arrived," he said coolly.

But he wasn't looking at Kim. Kim turned around and saw Amelia and her senior friends walking down the hall. Ron walked past Kim without even glancing at her.

"Amelia, let's lunch," he said.

"Okay," said Amelia. She took his arm. Together
they walked off down the hallway.

Kim shook her head sadly. "Oh, Pinky-Joe," she moaned.

Brrrrinnnng!

The bell for classes sounded. Up and down the school corridor, classroom doors opened. Kids spilled out into the hall.

At that moment, Rufus was walking down the middle of the hallway, looking for Ron. Suddenly, the floor began to tremble. The hallway was filling up with feet!

"Eeeeeeeep!" Rufus squealed. He leaped out of the way of a spiked heel. But he rolled right into the path of a high-top sneaker! Rufus squealed again. Ducking and dodging, he tried to find a way out of the chaos.

Just then, Rufus looked up. The sole of a huge work boot was about to squash him flat as a pancake!

"Eeeeeeeee!" Rufus squealed.

Suddenly, a hand swooped down and scooped him up. He was saved!

"Rufus!" Kim said. "What are you doing out here?"

Rufus looked around sadly. Kim realized that he was lost.

"Come on," she said. "Let's get you into Ron's locker."

But when Kim opened Ron's locker, she found a surprise. His shelves were crammed with combs, mirrors, and hair gels. There wasn't a single inch to spare for Rufus!

Kim had had it! The new Ron needed a wake-up call. Kim slammed the locker shut and stormed off to find him.

At that moment, Ron was sitting in the cafeteria, surrounded by a pack of girls. They sighed dreamily as Ron ran his fingers through his slick hair.

"Wow," said Amelia.

"Yes, Amelia, wow," Ron said. "The secret is the sea urchin."

"Excuse me . . . Ron?" Kim interrupted. Grabbing Ron by the shoulders, she yanked him out into the hall.

"What is with you?" she asked as they walked down the hallway. Well, *Kim* walked. *Ron* strutted.

"If you mean, am I the new Ron? Yes, I am," he said.

Kim pulled Rufus out of her pocket. "I

gotta say, I don't think the old Ron would've left Rufus on the floor," she said. "He was almost hallway roadkill."

Rufus blinked sadly at Ron. Didn't Ron care about him anymore?

"Rufus, you've gotta be more careful," Ron said. "What if something happened to you?"

"Awwww!" Rufus squeaked. Ron did love him! Squealing with joy, Rufus leaped toward Ron's head.

"Whoa, bro. Careful of the 'do," Ron said. He caught the little mole rat in midair and handed him back to Kim.

Kim's face turned an angry red. "So, there's no room for Rufus in your new life?" she asked furiously.

"Yes, there is," Ron said. "There's just no room for him in my new pants." He wiggled his hips to show off his shiny black trousers. "Pleather," he said. "You like?"

Before Kim could say anything, Amelia appeared. "Walk me to history, Ron?" she asked.

"Boo-yah!" said Ron, taking her arm. Without so much as a "Ciao for now," Ron hurried off down the hall with Amelia. Rufus watched him leave, stunned.

Poor Rufus, Kim thought. He looked like he'd just lost his best friend.

"Come on," she said. "You can live in *my* locker."

In Kim's locker, Rufus looked at the photo of goofy old Ron that was taped to her locker door. He whined sadly.

"Yeah," Kim agreed. "I liked him that way, too."

Suddenly, the monitor on Kim's computer lit up. It was Wade. And he didn't look happy.

"Kim, we've got trouble," he said. "Big-time trouble."

"What's the damage?" Kim asked.

"The damage is Señor Senior, Sr.," Wade said. "I thought you said he was harmless."

"Yeah," Kim replied. "Rich. But harmless."

Wade frowned. Señor Senior, Sr., didn't seem harmless any longer. "He's sucked up all the power in Western Europe," he explained.

Kim rolled her eyes. She'd gone to all that trouble to give the Seniors those eco-awareness pamphlets, and they hadn't even read them! "Okay, I'll go back and make sure he turns off some of his lights," she said.

"It's going to take more than that, Kim," Wade said seriously. "Señor Senior, Sr.'s taking Europe's power on purpose. Check this out."

A video of Señor Senior, Sr., appeared on Kim's computer screen. He had a sinister gleam in his eyes.

"My evil vow is this," Señor Senior, Sr., said to the camera. "I will send all of Europe back into the Dark Ages, unless the Euro Alliance gives me all of their nice little islands."

Kim blinked. "Nice little islands?" she

repeated. What kind of evil demand was that?

Señor Senior, Jr., danced onto the screen next to his father. "With the warm beach days and the hot disco nights," he said, just to make it clear.

Wade shook his head. "They are obviously new at the big-time villain thing," he said.

"That's what worries me," Kim replied. "I'll get Ron."

Grabbing Rufus, Kim slammed her locker door and rushed down the hallway. They had to save Europe!

CHAPTER 8

The Evil Lair

All of Europe was in darkness.

But on Señor Senior, Sr.'s island, every lightbulb in the house was blazing.

Inside his compound, Señor Senior, Sr., was reading his new villain manual called *The Book of Evil.*

"Hmmm, evil chortle . . ." he said, trying out an evil chortle. He sounded like a chicken with the flu. Not for me, he decided. He turned a page. "Ahh, the evil snicker."

Señor Senior, Sr., hunched up his shoulders and snickered evilly. It was so good, he even gave himself the shivers.

"That will do for now," he said, snapping the book shut. "Junior?" he called out to his son. "Any word from the Euro Alliance?"

"Somebody called—I don't know who," Junior replied. He drummed his fingers on the table and pouted. He was finding being a supervillain super*boring*.

"Did you think to take a message?" his father asked.

"I did not," Junior snapped. "I am not your message-taking person."

Señor Senior, Sr., scowled at his good-for-nothing son. "If you want your own island," he said, "you will think to take a message," he growled, slamming his fist down on the table.

Suddenly, he spotted something on the giant security monitor. Somebody was swimming toward the island! Make that *somebodies*. Señor Senior, Sr., watched as a duo in scuba suits crawled onto the rocky shore.

"Look, Ron Stoppable returns," he said to his son.

Junior peered at the screen. "Has he got the new trousers?" he asked.

"Yes," said Señor Senior, Sr.—"scuba trousers."

On the shore, Kim and Ron scrambled up the cliff until they could see the Seniors' compound.

"Whoa," Ron said, looking around. "He's been busy."

Señor Senior, Sr., *had* been busy. The twenty-foot wall was reinforced with extra steel and a double row of razor wire. Huge spotlights scanned the beach. Kim pulled Ron out of sight as one of the spotlights swept over them. Suddenly, she noticed something sticking out of the wall. It looked like a row of rockets.

"Oh, good," she snapped. "Missiles. I'm so glad you told him to get missiles."

Ron shrugged. "So I make a few suggestions. Does that make it my fault?" he asked.

"One hundred percent," Kim replied.

When the coast was clear, Kim and Ron dashed from behind the rocks, scaled the wall, and leaped to the ground on the other side.

There they heard a humming sound. Right in the center of the compound was the largest electrical plug they'd ever seen!

It glowed and hummed as waves of power surged through it.

"Is that what I think it is?" Ron asked.

"That's how he's draining the power," Kim said. "Come on. Let's get this settled." She turned toward the Seniors' lair.

"How're you planning on getting inside?" Ron asked, pulling her back.

"Through the door," Kim said. Marching up to the front door, she pounded against it with her fist. "Señor Senior, Sr.!" she shouted.

Whoosh! The doors slid open. Kim and Ron stepped inside.

"Kim Possible," said a voice overhead. "Welcome."

Kim looked up. Señor Senior, Sr., was standing on a catwalk high above them. He held a book in one hand. "I've been—"

"Hey!" Ron interrupted. He pointed to a

stream of water flowing through the center of the living room. "You put in a lagoon!"

"The piranhas won't be here until Monday," Señor Senior, Sr., replied. "But I assure you the koi have not been fed in days."

Kim and Ron watched as a large fish leaped up and snapped the air in front of them. It *did* seem to be hungry.

Señor Senior, Sr., snickered evilly and held up a villainous-looking manual. "I ordered a book on world domination off the Internet," he explained. "It said you'd be coming back."

But Kim wasn't impressed. It would take more than a little Web shopping to scare her away. "Have you gotten to the part where you give yourself up?" she asked.

"Actually, I'm up to the part where I tell you that it's too late for you to stop my evil plan," the villain replied.

"Oh, man!" Ron suddenly moaned. Kim glanced over at him. His eyes were crossed. He was looking at a red dot in the middle of his face. "I have a zit on my nose!" he complained.

"Ron, will you get over yourself?" Kim snapped.

"You do, too," Ron said, pointing to a red dot that had suddenly appeared on Kim's forehead. "Right there."

Kim touched her forehead. Suddenly, she realized what it was.

"Self-activating lasers!" she yelled. Kim grabbed Ron and dove for cover just as two laser beams fired at them. The beams blasted a hole in the concrete floor.

"'Throw in some traps,'" Kim said, mimicking Ron.

"Hey, on the positive side," Ron said. "This guy is clearly a terrific listener."

"Kim Possible!" Señor Senior, Sr., called. "Here's a good target. I'm going to attack your hometown."

A map of the United States suddenly appeared on the monitor. A red dot glowed on the city of Middleton.

"Junior, go to the tower and activate the missiles," Señor Senior, Sr., commanded.

"Oh, now I'm your missile-launching person, too," Junior whined. Throwing his hands in the air, he ran down the catwalk and disappeared through a doorway.

"Junior just split," Ron told Kim.

Kim nodded. "I'll deal with Senior," she said. "You go after Junior."

As Ron started off, Kim pulled Rufus from her pocket and gently set him on the ground. "Keep an eye on him," she told Rufus. "The old Ron may still be inside there somewhere."

She watched as Rufus chased after Ron. The two ran across the room, dodging laser fire until suddenly—*pow!* A laser blast hit right at Ron's feet! It was so close that it burned a hole in his fancy new leather boots.

"Ahhh!" Ron yelled. He ducked behind a wall. The lasers had cut off his path. Now there was only one way out—across the lagoon.

Taking a deep breath, Ron raced for the lagoon. Skidding and sliding, he made his way across a path of slippery rocks. Hungry koi jumped from the water, snapping at his ankles.

Rufus was right behind him. The fearsome fish flew at him from all sides. But Rufus knocked them down with powerful  kicks from his little legs.

At last, Ron and Rufus made it to the other side. *Whoosh!* The sliding door opened, and they disappeared through it. They were safe for now.

Kim sighed with relief, but then realized

she was covered with red dots. Every laser cannon in the room was aimed at her! With a mighty leap, Kim dove out of the way. The laser beams blasted a hole in the floor the size of a crater.

Kim zigzagged across the room. The lasers followed her every move. But Kim was quick. She stayed one step ahead of them as she climbed higher and higher up the walls. When she was almost to the cannons, Kim pushed off. She spun through the air in a triple back flip. *Pow! Pow! Pow!* Laser beams crisscrossed the room, when suddenly . . .

Kaboom! The cannons exploded! They had fired on one another!

Kim tumbled to the floor. But no sooner had she jumped to her feet than she heard Señor Senior, Sr., laugh.

"Oh, you think you're out of trouble?" he asked. "Well, you're not. Farewell, Kim Possible."

He pushed a button on a remote control. *Whoosh!* A door in the wall slid open. A whirring noise echoed through the hall.

Suddenly, a six-foot-tall metal top spun

into the room. Spikes jutted from its sides like the teeth of a giant saw.

"Spinning Tops of Doom!" Kim gasped. She watched in horror as the top whirled into a potted palm. In seconds, the tree was sawdust.

Whoosh! Another door slid open, and another Spinning Top of Doom whizzed out. Kim managed to somersault out of the way just in time. She ran for a door.

But two more Tops of Doom blocked her path. There was no way out. Kim was trapped.

CHAPTER 9

Hair Duel

Meanwhile, up in the missile tower, Señor Senior, Jr., was getting ready to blow Middleton to kingdom come.

"Why do I have to launch these stupid missiles?" he grumbled as he punched the controls. He hated doing anything that didn't involve getting a tan.

Junior flipped a switch, and the missile compartments opened. The missile heads pointed toward Middleton. They were almost ready to launch!

69

Suddenly, Ron burst through the door. "Step away from the console!" he shouted.

Junior glanced up and frowned. "Step away from your bossy attitude," he said. "You think just because you're so nicely dressed—*oooph!*" Junior flew backward as Ron tackled him to the ground.

The two rolled across the floor, wrestling. Ron had almost pinned Junior when, suddenly, Junior reached out and . . . messed up Ron's hair!

"Aaaah!" Ron shrieked. He let go of Junior and leaped to his feet. Whipping a comb from his pocket, he frantically began to restyle his hair.

Meanwhile, Junior was back at the console. He started programming the missiles.

Ron had to do something! He rushed up behind Junior and messed up *his* hair.

"Aaaaaah!" Junior screamed. He jumped back from the console and expertly redid his 'do. Ron saw his chance. He leaped at the controls and began to deprogram the missiles.

Back and forth, the two fought angrily. But Junior stepped over the line when he snatched Ron's comb from his hand and snapped it in half.

Then Junior whipped out a comb of his own and was just about to fix his hair when Ron lunged  forward and grabbed his arm. For a moment they stood locked in combat.

At that moment, Rufus scurried into the tower. He saw Ron and Junior fighting over the comb. Rufus growled. This haircut thing had gone way too far!

With a grunt, Junior flipped Ron over. As his arm hit the ground, the comb flew from his hand. Ron and Junior watched, horrified, as it spun across the tower deck. It came to a stop on the very edge. Hundreds of feet below, waves crashed against the island's rocky cliffs.

Ron and Junior both lunged for the comb. Just then, Ron caught a glimpse of himself in the chrome wall. Beneath his perfect haircut, his face was red and sweating. Ron stared in horror at his reflection.

"Look at me. What have I become?" he said.

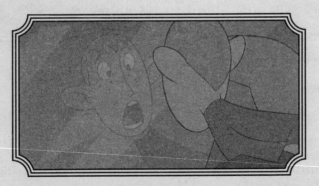

Just then, Rufus leaped onto Ron's head. He messed up Ron's hair one last time. Ron looked at his reflection. His old hair was back!

"My Ron-ness . . . I feel it. Yeah, this look works," he said happily.

"What 'look'? Let me see." Junior grabbed Ron's head and examined it. "But your hair is all messy," he said in surprise. "It is so . . . so . . ."

"Totally me," Ron said with relief.

Suddenly, they heard a whistle. Junior looked up just in time to see Rufus kick his comb over the edge. It tumbled down to the sharp rocks below.

Junior gasped and dove after it, almost falling over the edge.

"Whoa!" Ron said. He grabbed Junior's arm and pulled him back. "The stairs. Use the stairs."

Junior turned and fled down the stairs to find his comb. Ron went to work and deprogrammed the missiles. Middleton was saved!

But Kim was still in trouble.

CHAPTER 10

The Room of Doom

Bzzzzzzzzzzzzzzzzzzz! A Spinning Top of Doom whirled at Kim. She leaped out of the way. But a second later, another top came tearing toward her. Kim dodged again. The top sawed through the wall behind her.

Up on the catwalk, Señor Senior, Sr., snickered. It was only a matter of minutes before Kim would be too exhausted to dodge the spinning tops. She would be mincemeat!

Just then, Ron ran into the room. He had to

leap out of the way to avoid being sliced by a spinning top. The top plowed into a metal railing behind him.

Another top spun toward Kim, but she was too tired to move. Ron saw that she was in trouble. Thinking quickly, he grabbed one of the bars from the destroyed railing.

"Get down!" he screamed at Kim.

Kim ducked. Ron threw the metal bar and hit the top. It lost its balance. That gave Ron just enough time to pull Kim into the corner.

"Thanks," Kim said with a gasp.

The top was still spinning wildly out of control. It crashed into another top and exploded.

The blast knocked the other tops off course. They veered around the room, plowing into walls. At last the spinning tops came to a stop and fell over on their sides.

Señor Senior, Sr., gasped as the catwalk crumpled. He tumbled to the ground and dashed away.

For a moment, the room was silent. Kim and Ron slowly poked their heads up. The room was full of smoking wreckage.

Kim turned to Ron. "Never, never tell anyone to go out and buy Spinning Tops of Doom," she said. "You gotta be careful about what you say, Ron. I mean, one little thing . . ."

"Like 'you need a new hairstyle'?" Ron interrupted.

"Yeah," Kim said sheepishly. "Like that. Sorry."

"You know what the worst thing is?" Ron asked.

"What?" Kim asked.

Ron pointed to his pants. "Pleather doesn't breathe," he said.

Suddenly, they heard the roar of an engine. Kim and Ron ran to the window. Señor Senior, Sr., and Señor Senior, Jr., were racing away in a speedboat.

Kim chuckled. "Secret grotto and a speedboat," she said. "Great for escapes."

Ron winced. The Seniors had followed his suggestions right down to the getaway boat. "I am so not talking to anyone ever again," he moaned.

Kim smiled. "C'mon," she said. "Let's ace this place."

With their arms around each other's shoulders, the two friends headed home.

The New Old Ron

The old Ron was back and better than ever! The next morning, Ron came to school wearing dirty sneakers, a fuzzy red sweater, and his good old baggy cargo pants. It sure did feel good to be out of that pleather!

"You know," Ron said to Kim. "It wasn't really the haircut that made me popular."

Kim nodded.

"What people saw was confidence," Ron

went on. "So I ditch the haircut, keep the confidence."

Just then, Ron spotted Amelia and her friends. This was his chance to try out his new cool!

"Hey, Amelia," he said confidently. "We still on for after school?"

"After school with *you*?" Amelia looked at Ron like he was a squashed bug. "And do what? Geek out?"

Ron's face fell. "C'mon, it's me," he said. "Ron. So I ditched the 'do. It's what's inside that matters."

Amelia wrinkled her nose. "Like, who told you that, loser?" she said. With a flip of her hair she walked away. Ron sadly shuffled back to Kim.

Poor Ron, Kim thought. Well, there was only one thing left to do. Kim opened her locker. With a squeal of joy, Rufus leaped out. He landed right on Ron.

Kim smiled. "See," she said. "Someone likes you just the way you are."

Ron smiled, too, happy to be himself again.